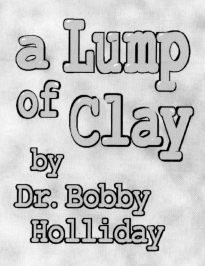

a Lump of Clay
by
Dr. Bobby Holliday

LADY HAWK PRESS

A Division of Equus Enterprises, Inc.
www.ladyhawkpress.com

ISBN 978-0-9829082-1-1

Printed in the United States by BookMasters, Inc.,
30 Amberwood Parkway, Ashland, OH 44805
No. M7907, November 2010

**Cover, Illustrations and Book Design
by Rebecca Price
www.rebeccaprice.com**

Foreword

Three years ago, Dr. Holliday had an idea for a children's book. She used to work at a potter's wheel in high school creating many different types of pottery. Her favorite was one of her first pieces that was so heavy that it was really not very useful. The memory of this imperfect-but-loved anyway creation inspired the idea for th   oo   *A Lump* of Clay.

Dedication

To Moses

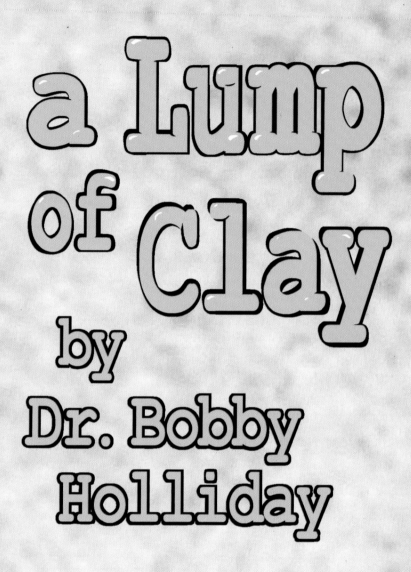

a Lump
of Clay
by
Dr. Bobby
Holliday

Illustrated by Rebecca Price

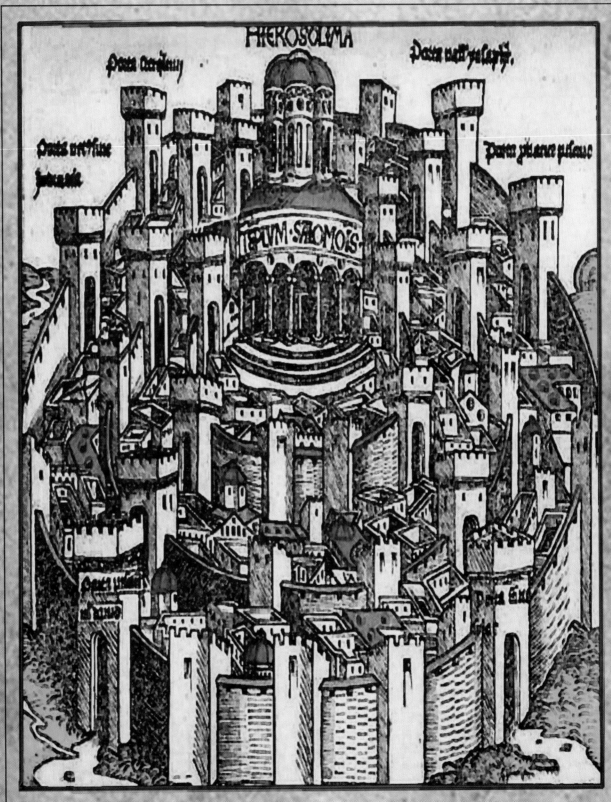

JERUSALEM

In the city of Jerusalem, near the Western Wall of the old city of King David, there lived the most renowned potter in all the land; Manasseh the Forgetful. Now Manasseh was a very old man and didn't mean to be forgetful, but it was just that he started so many projects and was distracted so easily that he had earned the title many, many years before...when a remarkable set of events happened...

It all began the day Manasseh was getting ready to make one of his many famous and very expensive potteries for none other than the great King Herod himself. Manasseh had been commissioned by the King to make a centerpiece for the Royal Table. King Herod wanted this centerpiece to go down in history as one of the most unusual and special centerpieces that had ever been created. He wanted everyone in the land to talk about his centerpiece for many years to come.

Manasseh was very excited that he had been commissioned to do this great work of art and was eager to please the king. He very carefully took a large amount of his special secret clay to make into something for the king's Royal Table—not too large an amount, but larger than it would usually take to make a centerpiece for just any table. Manasseh thought out loud, "Well, if this is going to be for the king's table, then why should I spare any expense to make it the best that I can possibly make? It is the king, right? Who is more important than the king? I want the whole land to speak of this creation for many, many years, so I should make it bigger than anything I have made in the past!" Manasseh was set on making something so big, so unusual and so special that everyone had to notice, right? He asked, "Wasn't that the sign of greatness? Wasn't that what a king would want? Something large? Something pleasing to the eye?"

So Manasseh took the large lump of clay and placed it on his potter's wheel to begin his great impressive centerpiece for King Herod.

A Lump of Clay by Dr. Bobby Holliday

Unbeknownst to Manasseh the Forgetful, the lump of clay had overheard the potter as he was talking to the king's spokesperson about the great centerpiece.

He was so very excited when the potter took him out of the special bag of clay that all the other potters coveted. He was part of the special clay that Manasseh only used for very special occasions to make very special pieces. His mind was running wild with possibilities of what he was going to become at the experienced hands of Manasseh the famous potter.

He boasted, "Why, I am going to be the envy of all the other potteries! Everyone will be looking at me in awe, talking about me all over Jerusalem. Everyone will know about my outward beauty. I will be legendary, my importance unparalleled!"

Manasseh, with the lump of clay carefully placed right in the center of his potter's wheel, took in a deep breath and prayed, "Lord, this piece belongs to You and You only. Please guide my hands to make something beautiful for Your eyes and Your eyes alone. This honor to make a piece for a king is a great honor, but You, Lord, are higher than any man or king on earth, and I want this piece to be pleasing unto You."

With that prayer, Manasseh began to turn the wheel and the lump of clay, to his delight, grew higher and higher in the care of his experienced hands. He twirled and twirled with great care as the wheel turned around and around and around. The lump of clay was thrilled and so was Manasseh.

All of a sudden, a mysterious great wind arose out of nowhere blowing all the trees so they swayed in its power. The huge wind knocked all the shutters open in his house all at the same time and blew in his front door too.

This mysterious wind blew in leaves from the trees all over his floor and then stopped as quickly as it came. Manasseh, a bit confused, went outside to see what all this commotion was about, but no one else seemed to have noticed!

He was surprised that he was the only one that seemed to feel the effects of this mysterious wind that left as fast as it came. His neighbors thought he was mad, as they didn't feel any wind at all! He stayed outside talking with his neighbors about this mysterious wind, completely forgetting about his masterpiece for the king.

After almost an hour, Manasseh the Forgetful remembered his mission and quickly returned to his house to complete the masterpiece that he had started for King Herod.

Now, while all this commotion was going on and the potter was gone from his home, the lump of clay was busy day dreaming about what an extraordinary piece he was going to become and how famous he would be sitting on the king's table. He said to himself, "Will I be a beautiful glazed bowl of many colors? Will I be something so extraordinary that I will travel from city to city to be put on display? Maybe I will even travel on a camel and be protected by none other than the king's army? Will I hold many beautiful flowers placed daily upon me to adorn my beauty? Dare I think about how bright my future is?" He was so very excited about all these possibilities that he didn't seem to notice how long Manasseh had been gone. All he knew is that he was going to be outwardly beautiful and famous in the eyes of all the men in the Kingdom.

When the potter was finished shutting his shutters and sweeping his floor, everything seemed calm again, but he swore that he heard a voice, a very still, small voice, quietly speaking to his heart,

"The Lord uses the ordinary and humble things in life to accomplish His purposes—not the mighty and proud."

He didn't understand why this was going through his heart when he sat down to finish his masterpiece.

By the time Manasseh the Forgetful finally got back to his potter's wheel, he discovered that he had been gone far too long and there was no way that he was going to be able to salvage the piece that he had intended to make! He was heartbroken. He said, "Oy, there is nothing that I can do other than to take most of the special clay from this piece and throw it away! It is all dried up and no longer useable. Now, all I will have left is just enough to make a simple chalice."

His heart was very heavy at this prospect. He had such a deep feeling that this particular lump of clay was to be of great value to the King of Kings, our Lord God.

The lump of clay, upon hearing Manasseh speak out loud of this loss, was devastated. He cried, "How could I have gone from greatness to being destitute in just the space of minutes? How can I sit on the potter's shelf along with his other great creations just being a simple ordinary chalice that anyone could make! No one will want me now. How could this have happened to me?"

He screamed, "Just throw me away with the rest of the dried up clay! I don't want to live my life as just another ordinary piece living my life in humility and shame now that I am not worthy of the king's table. I have already told everyone how great I was going to be! How can I face them now?"

The potter fashioned the now little lump of clay into a simple chalice. He glazed the chalice with an ordinary golden glaze and set him upon his shelf along with his prized creations still believing that this simple golden chalice was still special in some way. He took another lump of his special clay to make the centerpiece for the King.

The lump of clay was heartbroken at what he had become. All the other potteries made fun of him and ridiculed him for his boasting and pride when he thought he was going to be famous. They teased, "Oh, let us all bow down to the mighty and great king's centerpiece, Ha ha ha. Look at you now. You're nothing but a simple golden chalice. You are not even worthy of being on the same shelf as us!"

The golden chalice sat for months and months on the potter's shelf enduring the teasing and snide remarks slowly feeling more and more depressed as each day went by with no one wanting him. No one even noticed him and no one thought he was special in any way. He was just ordinary. He was less than ordinary in his mind. He just wanted someone to love him and forgive him of his past prideful behavior.

One day, the Potter's nephew, Mark, came into the store. He was staying at his aunt's house in Jerusalem. Manasseh the Forgetful forgot who he was! Once he finally remembered, he was a little embarrassed and wanted to give him a gift that meant something to him, so he reached up and took the little golden chalice down from the shelf and gave it to Mark.

He told him that the golden chalice was very special to him. Mark thanked his uncle for the gift, as he knew he was a famous potter in Jerusalem, not only for the pottery that he created, but also for being a gracious and merciful person. He loved the little golden chalice because Manasseh had given it freely to him.

Mark decided that the best thing for him to do with his gift from Manasseh was to give the golden chalice to his aunt for her hospitality. She let him stay there for just doing some little tasks for her once in a while and Mark was grateful to her. Mark's aunt loved her gift from her nephew and put the golden chalice with the rest of her nicest dishes in her cupboard.

Her friends haughtily remarked, "She is just being compassionate toward her nephew's modest gift. This chalice certainly doesn't belong with the other great pieces in her cupboard. I can't believe Manasseh the Forgetful even made this piece of junk. Perhaps he forgot what he was doing! Well, I certainly wouldn't have that in my cupboard."

The golden chalice overheard what they said but he didn't mind at all. He knew that she loved him and that is all that mattered to him now.

Three months later, Mark's aunt asked him to prepare the upper room in her house for Passover. Mark had never been asked to prepare the room before and he took his responsibility seriously.

While he was setting the table, he remembered the chalice that he had given his aunt that she loved so much. In the traditional seating in Jerusalem, there was a seat reserved for the host. It was the second seat in from the aisle on a u-shaped table. Mark placed this very golden chalice, this little lump of clay, at the seat of the host of the Passover.

He felt that this was the very chalice that should be there even though he really couldn't explain why. He remembered that Manasseh had said this chalice was special when he gave it to him even though it was not impressive like his other works. Somehow, Mark knew that this night was not to be like any other night...

The next morning, Mark's aunt asked him to go fetch water in a pitcher from the well in the middle of town. Mark thought this was a strange request as the women usually carried the pitchers of water from the well. She had never asked him to do this before, but Mark didn't mind. His aunt had been very kind to him, so off to the well he went.

After he had gotten the pitcher of water, he noticed two men following him all the way back to his aunt's house. When they saw her, they said, "The Teacher says, where is my guest room in which I may eat the Passover with my disciples?" **(Mathew 26:18)**

Mark was instructed to show the two men the upper room that he had prepared for the Passover.

When evening came, Mark knew whom the Passover table had been prepared for; it was for Jesus of Nazareth and His twelve disciples!! He knew that Jesus had come to town riding on the foal of a donkey, but he had no idea that Jesus Christ himself would be in his very home! He waited around the corner of the stairs to see if he could catch a glimpse of Jesus. When he saw him coming, his heart almost burst with excitement.

He watched as Jesus sat down to the very table that he had prepared and drank from the very same golden chalice that he had so lovingly placed there.

Mark listened as Jesus took some of the bread, and after a blessing, broke it and gave it to the disciples. He said, "Take, eat; this My body." **(Matthew 26:26)**. Then Jesus took the little golden chalice and gave thanks. He passed the golden chalice to his disciples saying, "Drink from it, all of you; for this is my blood of the covenant, which is poured out for many for forgiveness of sins" **(Matthew 26:28)**. The golden chalice was passed around the table for all the twelve to take a sip of the wine it held. "But I say to you, I will not drink of this fruit of the vine from now until that day when I drink it anew with you in my Father's kingdom" **(Matthew 26:29)**.

When the golden chalice realized what was taking place and who was at the head of this Passover dinner, he was speechless! He thought, "Who am I that I am at the head of this most important dinner with none other than the King of all Kings, Jesus Christ!!" He was so humbled that he felt that he did not deserve such an extraordinary honor. Not him, not after all the things he had done.

Now this was quite a turn around from the days when he was first taken out of the special bag of clay by Manasseh the Forgetful. The golden chalice had been on the potter's shelf for so long and had endured being the object of ridicule from the other fine pieces of pottery in Mark's aunt's cupboard for so long, that he had lost all of his former pride. He had healed from the pain and hurt of not becoming what he had dreamed of becoming. Instead, he spent his days counting his blessings, but there was always this nagging feeling that he wanted to be forgiven for his former sins. When he heard the words that Jesus said at the Passover, he wept to himself.

He knew that Jesus had forgiven him for his pride and arrogance. He knew that Jesus loved him. He also knew that tonight was not like any other night...

The golden chalice realized that this was the whole point all along. Jesus didn't want a prideful chalice to drink from that night. He wanted a humbled, grateful, content chalice. What the golden chalice did not know is that from that night on he would go down in history as 'The Holy Grail'. He would be famous after all, only not for his outward beauty, but for his humble gentle spirit and pureness of heart.

To this date, no one knows where the golden chalice may be hiding. Many have tried to find him. Many have failed. My guess is that he is happily in someone's cupboard along with all the other pieces of ordinary pottery feeling blessed because he can be useful and that he is loved. He had learned to be satisfied in whatever circumstances God chose to put him in.

When Manasseh the Forgetful heard of the tale of his golden chalice from his nephew Mark, he had forgotten all about making the centerpiece for King Herod! What he did remember is that he always thought that the lump of clay that he had taken out of the bag on that day many, many years ago was meant for something very special. He always remembered that still small voice that spoke to his heart that very same day saying,

"The Lord uses the ordinary and humble things
in life to accomplish His purposes—not the mighty
and proud."

Bobby and Calgary

For more information about Dr. Bobby Holliday, visit:
www.bobbyholliday.biz

About the Author

Dr. Bobby Holliday possesses a PhD in Clinical Psychology with a minor in Theology. Her dissertation was written on "The Effects Of Equine Therapy For People With Mental Or Physical Disabilities", which allowed her the privilege to work with many disabled children during the months it took to complete the dissertation work. She is an equestrian and her love for horses has given her the desire to create an Equine Therapy program that caters to children with disabilities, and veterans returning from the front lines.

A Lump Of Clay is the first in a series of books about people and animals of the bible. It is her hope that these books can be used by God as an inspirational message to children and as a teaching tool for some of the basic principles in the Christian faith.

Dr. Holliday's work as a voice-over actor signed with William Morris Endeavor Entertainment not only supported her through college, it also gave her a unique perspective on the language styles and rhythms that children of all ages respond to.

For news and previews of
Dr Holliday's upcoming books, visit:
www.ladyhawkpress.com

Narration CD for A Lump of Clay

CREDITS

CD VOICES

MANASSEH, TEASING POTTERIES, DISCIPLE, JESUS
RECORDED BY: RODGER BUMPASS

NARRATION, LUMP OF CLAY, TEASING POTTERIES, HAUGHTY
WOMEN
RECORDED BY: BOBBY HOLLIDAY

LUMP OF CLAY SONG
WRITTEN AND RECORDED BY: BOBBY HOLLIDAY

MICAH JOHNSON, SOUND ENGINEER
ATLANTIS RECORDING GROUP